*A Very Weird
and Moogly Christmas*

A Very Weird and Moogly Christmas

PATRICIA WINDSOR

A Yearling Book

Published by
Dell Publishing
a division of
Bantam Doubleday Dell Publishing Group, Inc.
666 Fifth Avenue
New York, New York 10103

ISBN: 0-440-40528-9

Printed in the United States of America

November 1991

10 9 8 7 6 5 4 3 2 1

OPM

With love to
Police Officer Frank Hickey
and
my cousin Kathleen Wills

A Very Weird
and Moogly Christmas

1.

Martha woke up very early and didn't know where she was. It was scary for a moment, and then she remembered. She was in her room at the Belleflower Hotel. Even with the window closed, she could hear the sound of the sea. She pulled the blanket up over her head to drown it out.

But she couldn't breathe, and had to come up for air. Milky white dawn was coming through the curtains. Martha got out of bed and went to the window, wondering if that strange thing would be out there again.

She could see the long stretch of beach, cold and lonely looking, beyond the dunes outside the hotel. A couple of sea gulls screeched and landed. Martha waited, her bare feet turning to ice.

There it was! Dark and raggedy as a pile of dirty laundry, it scuttled along like an awkward crab, scattering the gulls that were scavenging on the sand. Martha watched until it had disappeared up the beach.

What was it? she thought, hurrying back to bed and jumping under the blankets to warm up her toes. A person or some strange sea creature that only came out at dawn? At least now she knew she wasn't dreaming, because she'd seen the strange figure two mornings in a row. She wondered if anyone else noticed, but probably they were all still sleeping. Except for Teddy, and she wasn't sure about telling him. Teddy had changed.

Besides, it was Teddy's fault she was here at Delaware Beach in the middle of winter, so she was feeling a little grumpy toward him. Christmas was in three days, the first she would spend away from home. Nothing about it would seem private and just for the family. Instead, they'd have to share the hotel tree with the other guests and get dressed before they could come down to open presents. It would be weird not opening presents in pajamas. It would be the weirdest Christmas ever.

Of course, Teddy thought all of it was great. Martha thought it would be a lot greater in the summer, when normal people came to the beach. Last summer Teddy and his mother had come for a vacation, staying right here in the Belleflower Hotel. Teddy's mother, Mrs. Winterrab, liked it so much, she said she wished she could stay all year round. That's when she found out the hotel was for sale. And she bought it. Teddy had come back and bragged about it to everyone. Martha had felt a little grumpy with him then, too, because he'd never once said he was sorry to be leaving Melody Woods.

Martha had missed him a lot, especially when school started. It felt strange not to see Teddy at lunch, eating his peanut-butter-and-banana sandwiches. When Mrs. Winterrab wrote to offer special low Christmas rates to all the people in Melody Woods, Martha was excited. She could hardly believe it when her parents decided to come. Even more astonishing was the fact that her older sister, Jemima, wanted to come too. Usually, Jemima would have screamed the house down about leaving her friends, but it happened that she'd decided to break up with her boyfriend, Mellow, just before Christmas vacation began. She jumped at the chance to have a place to hide out, because she had no dates for the holiday parties.

Well, it had all seemed like a terrific idea, until Martha arrived and found Teddy acting all hustle and bustle, just like Martha's dad, with his head full of business. Neither the beach nor Teddy was turning out to be much fun. And never once had he even said he'd missed her.

Martha sighed and rolled over and shut her eyes. She'd try to get a little more sleep before Teddy came banging on her door, urging her to get up so they could go out on the beach to see if the waves had frozen. He was overly enthusiastic about everything that had to do with the beach and right now it was frozen waves. Martha supposed she should try to be a better friend and not act so grumpy. But it was hard. She had never thought she would feel homesick. She wondered how Margaret the cat felt, spending Christmas without them. Phyllis Blott had promised to take good care of her, but Martha bet Margaret was going to run away from home permanently after this.

"Keep a stiff upper lip" was what Dad said sometimes. It meant you were not supposed to start blubbering when things got tough. Martha thought it was pretty dumb advice, probably the worst her dad had ever given. If you couldn't blubber when you were unhappy, when could you blubber?

It was no use. She could not go back to sleep. She kicked off the blankets and sat up. It was still early, a good time to use the bathroom before Jemima took over. Martha put on her robe and opened her door. The hall was empty and quiet except for the ticking of the big clock at the end. She crept down to the bathroom and shut herself in. Then she had a good blubber, without anyone hearing, because she turned on the water full force.

2.

"Have another blueberry pancake, lovey," said Mrs. Plum, the hotel's cook.

Martha had already eaten four. "Okay," she said, more to wipe the worried expression from Mrs. Plum's brow than because she was still hungry.

As Teddy's personal friend, Martha got to eat in the hotel kitchen with him. All the other guests had meals in the dining room. Martha liked not having to sit with Mom and Dad and Jemima. They were always so jolly in the morning, something that never happened at home. And Jemima acted like she was a rich person on an ocean liner, talking in a phony stuck-up voice and trying to order all kinds of special things that weren't on the menu. Martha preferred the cozy kitchen. As Mrs. Plum bustled at the big stove, whipping up hot breakfasts for the hotel guests, she told them all kinds of funny stories. This morning Martha felt in a half-and-half mood: half grouchy, half okay. But Mrs. Plum's pancakes were making it mostly okay.

"Now, what have you two got on the agenda for today?" Mrs. Plum asked, ladling perfect poached eggs onto a tray of toast and bacon.

"First, we're going to check on the waves," said Teddy.

Mrs. Plum sniffed the air as if she could smell the outside weather in spite of the hot, steamy kitchen. "Perhaps not today," she said. "Not cold enough."

As far as Martha was concerned, the beach was plenty cold enough. Beaches were supposed to be hot and you were supposed to wear your bathing suit, not your down jacket, mittens, and boots.

"Waves can't possibly freeze," Martha said.

"Ah, lovey, don't count on it," said Mrs. Plum as she shoved the laden tray through the swinging door into the ample arms of her daughter, Petal. "I remember when we had a big freeze-up, and in the morning the waves had been caught in the act of tumbling. It looked as if someone had sculpted a ruffle all along the edge of the shore."

"They want more coffee, Mum," Petal said, coming back with the empty tray. "And another basket of sweet rolls."

Petal Plum was a strapping girl, much taller than her mother and a little older than Jemima. She had big freckled arms and legs and wore her sturdy shoes without stockings or socks even in the winter. Petal was always too hot and fanning herself. Her wiry red hair was clipped up on the top of her head so it wouldn't get into the food. She looked nothing like a petal. Martha thought the name Petal Plum was a riot and it was hard not to laugh when Teddy's mother went around saying that Mrs. Plum and Petal were perfect peaches. Teddy said, in his serious way, that reliable hotel help was hard to get these days and so they shouldn't make fun. Teddy said he was an expert in the hotel business. Sometimes Mrs. Plum even let him make his chocolate brownie cake for the guests' dessert.

"See, I told you waves could freeze," Teddy said smugly. "Even Mrs. Plum says so."

"You have to watch out then," Petal said. "Frozen waves is a sure sign of moogly times."

"None of that," Mrs. Plum reprimanded, handing Petal the filled coffeepot. "Get back to the guests."

"What did she mean by moogly?" Teddy asked.

Mrs. Plum shrugged. "I haven't a clue. Petal's head is full of stuff and nonsense. Now, how about some nice strawberry jam to help you finish up those pancakes?"

"You know what?" Martha said when Mrs. Plum had disappeared into the larder to fetch the jam. "It's boring not having to do anything."

She didn't have to make her bed, clean her room, or help with the dishes. Jemima loved it but it made Martha feel kind of empty. Having chores made a day seem right.

"I'll tell you what's boring," Teddy said. "Your being in a bad mood all the time."

"Who, me?" Martha was startled. She knew she was being a grouch, but she hadn't expected anyone to really notice.

"And you're always mad at me."

"I am?"

"Your sister, Jemima, is a lot more fun these days. And that's saying a lot, because I always thought she was a ditz."

Martha didn't know whether to come to Jemima's defense or her own. But before she could comment,

Teddy made a suggestion. "I know what will relieve your boredom. I'll give you a tour of the boardwalk. You haven't seen that yet."

Martha perked up a little. It sounded like fun. The boardwalk would be a lively place with cotton candy and rides and games they could play. "It sounds great," she told Teddy.

Looking pleased, Teddy wiped up the remains of his egg with a bit of toast. Then he carried his and Martha's plate to the sink.

"Go and brush your teeth," he said bossily, "and I'll meet you in the front hall."

"Yes, sir," Martha said, not too grumpily. At least now there was *something* to do.

As Martha was getting her toothbrush and toothpaste from her room, she heard a creak of footsteps in the hall. She hoped it wasn't Jemima. She'd want to tag along. Teddy might think Jemima was fun these days, but mostly she spent her time looking out for boys. If one came along, Jemima got all funny and was impossible to talk to.

But Jemima's room was empty, as Martha could plainly see as she walked past. That was the one good thing that had happened when they first arrived at Delaware Beach. Because it was off season, Mrs. Winterrab said she and Jemima could have separate rooms.

Martha dutifully brushed her teeth and carefully wiped off the sink before she left the bathroom. There was a framed sign on the wall, asking guests to leave the bathroom neat and tidy. Everyone cooperated except Jemima, who left hair in the sink and makeup smears all over the mirror.

As Martha walked back to her room, she noticed something funny. The velvet drape at the end of the hall was moving. Martha didn't much like the idea of that. It was a spooky drape, hiding a narrow, twisting staircase that went up to the attics. It was there to keep out drafts and it was old and sort of moldy, having been in the house for a long time before Mrs. Winterrab had come. Martha always hurried past it when she had to. Teddy said the attics were huge, room after room filled with all kinds of junk. But when Martha asked if they could explore, Teddy said no, they weren't allowed, it was one of his mother's rules.

Who would be going up in the attic now? Everyone was down at breakfast, including Mrs. Winterrab, who liked to sit and chat with her guests in the dining room. Mrs. Plum and Petal were always busy for at least an hour after the breakfast rush, cleaning up the dining room and kitchen. Jerry or Ben would be at the desk or working in the office. And the extra cleaning people only came later in the day.

Martha hurried back to her room, got her outdoor clothes, and rushed out. She felt guilty. No matter how many times she told herself it was all right, she still couldn't get over not having to make her bed. She couldn't help pulling up the sheets and blankets anyway, but Petal always made it over again, stretching the sheets tight as boards and making it impossible to get your feet down between them at night.

Maybe it was just the wind, Martha thought as she went down the big old staircase. Except that the old moldy curtain was as heavy as lead and couldn't possibly blow in the wind.

"It's about time," Teddy said, waiting at the bottom of the stairs, tapping his foot and looking at his watch. "What a slowpoke. Do you know your sister's already been out for a jog? If there were any frozen waves, they've probably *un*frozen by now."

Martha decided not to tell him about the drape. Teddy was getting to be sort of a pain.

3.

They had to walk a few blocks through the town to get to the boardwalk. The narrow streets were lined with all kinds of interesting-looking shops. But all of them were closed for the winter.

"It's a lot of fun in the summer," Teddy said.

Martha thought it was like walking through a ghost town. "Doesn't anybody else live here?" she asked. "Did you make any friends at school?"

"Oh, sure," Teddy said.

"So, where are they?"

Teddy shrugged. "Away on vacation, I guess. A lot of people go away this time of year."

Martha decided not to ask anything more in case it made him feel bad. Maybe Teddy hadn't made any friends in the short time he had lived at the beach. Or maybe, like back home, the kids thought he was a weirdo. Anyway, she was looking forward to the boardwalk.

Of course, she should have known. The boardwalk was closed up, just like the shops. Big iron shutters were pulled down on all the arcades. Scraps of paper and old candy wrappers blew along the railings and empty benches.

"It must be a real fun place when it's open," Martha said, ready to go back to the hotel.

But Teddy led her along, pointing out the sights. He showed her where the big carousel went around from morning until night, and where they sold the world's best hot dogs. He told her how he'd won a game called Whack-a-Mole three times with the highest score.

Martha was horrified. "Whack a mole?" She had a vision of little animals being hit on the head.

"They're only plastic," Teddy explained. "They pop up and down out of their holes and you hit them with a mallet. I usually get 250 points and win a stuffed bear."

"Great," Martha said.

Suddenly Teddy yanked her arm. Before she knew it, she was being dragged down the boardwalk at a terrific pace. "What's going on?" she asked.

"Quick. In here," he said, and pulled her into a small opening in the long row of firmly closed shutters.

Martha glared at him as she caught her breath. Teddy held up a warning hand, then peered cautiously around the doorway.

"I think we gave him the slip."

"Who?" Martha puffed.

Teddy pushed his glasses back up his nose. "This kid from town."

"One of your new friends?"

"No! I don't know him at all, he's not in my school. He's just a pest."

Martha was surprised. It wasn't like Teddy to evade the issue. Martha was more the one to avoid people she didn't want to meet. Teddy always said you should face things. "He must be really awful," she said, hoping to hear the gory details.

Teddy seemed reluctant to discuss it. "He talks about lions all the time. And about lion teeth. His face is . . . kind of funny." Teddy looked perplexed, then gave himself an impatient shake. "He's just weird, that's all."

Martha laughed. "I guess it takes a weirdo to know a weirdo." Maybe that wasn't a good thing to say. Maybe in this new town he didn't have the same reputation for being a weirdo that he'd had back home.

Teddy was peering around the door again.

"Are we going to hide here all morning?" Martha asked.

"Just until the coast is clear."

Martha looked around the small space. Behind them was a wooden door with a small window and a black iron knocker in the shape of a bird. She was trying to figure out what kind of bird it was when Teddy said in alarm, "He's heading right for us!"

"Well, there's no place to go," Martha said.

"Unless . . ." She wondered what would happen if they knocked the knocker.

But it wasn't necessary to knock. In desperation Teddy gave the door a push and it creaked open.

"Quick," Teddy said, and shoved her inside. He shut the door behind them and it closed with an ominous click.

"Oh, rats!" Martha cried, then quickly lowered her voice to a whisper. "You locked us in."

"No, I didn't," he whispered back, and gave the

doorknob a careful tug to prove it. The door wouldn't budge. He smiled sheepishly. "Well, at least we escaped from *him*."

They were standing in a long, dark hallway cluttered with boxes. The place looked like it hadn't been occupied in a long time. There was some kind of funny smell.

"We could be stuck in here for years before somebody finds us," Martha said.

"Only for the winter. They'd find us in the summer."

"We'll be starved by then."

"Who's that?" asked a disembodied, inquiring voice.

They froze.

"Come in, don't stand out there in the dark." It wasn't a scary voice, Martha thought. More like the voice of a nice old lady.

"Come on," she told Teddy. "We have to find a way out anyway." It was her turn to do the dragging. She pulled him down the hall. "There's nothing to be afraid of," she said, noticing a mellow golden light up ahead.

But if it wasn't frightening, it certainly was disappointing. The room was full of faded furniture, pillows, draperies, fringed lamps, and cats. No nice old lady, just skinny, mean-looking cats. A small lamp with a yellow bulb was sending out the glow. In the center of the room was a big glass case that reminded Martha of the display cases at a museum. Inside it was an almost life-sized mechanical woman. She was dressed in a long purple silk gown. Her black hair, woven with

14

jewels, was piled high. She had glittery jet-black eyes, a dark red rosebud mouth, and big gold loops in her ears. Her little hands reached out as if to welcome them . . . or grab them. As they stared at her, a sudden groaning of machinery started up, sputtering, squeaking, and grating as if it needed some oil. The figure of the woman began to move its head from side to side and out came an uncanny tinny voice. *"Put in a penny, your fortune I shall tell."*

Teddy went closer to inspect. "I wonder where you put the money in."

"You're not going to do it?"

"It's a bargain. You can't buy much for a penny these days."

The mechanical doll sang again. Martha didn't like the way her eyes kept looking at them, almost as if they could really see. "I don't think it's a good idea."

"Why not?"

"Who wants to know bad news before it happens?"

"Oh, it's only a game. It'll tell us we'll be millionaires or live to be a hundred. It's not real."

"Then why bother? Come on, let's find a way out."

"Don't be so nervous," Teddy said, giving her a disgusted look. "This morning you were complaining you had nothing to do. Now here we are, having a little excitement, and you're still a mess." He shook his head. "I don't know what's come over you."

"The beach has come over me, that's what," Martha snapped. "If I could tell my own fortune, I'd wish myself back in Melody Woods."

Teddy looked hurt. "What's so great about there?"

"It's where I live."

15

He glared. "Well, this is where *I* live!"

Martha felt ashamed. She was about to apologize when the voice began its singsong again. *"Put in a penny . . ."*

"Oh, shut up," Martha said. To her surprise the doll stopped whirring and came to a stop with its head a-tilt.

"Now look what you've done," Teddy exclaimed.

"I didn't do anything," Martha said. "If you stick in a penny, it's sure to start again."

Teddy finally located the slot, but then he had to search his pockets for a penny. Martha told herself to be patient and let him get it over with, but the smell of cats was giving her a headache. She liked cats—after all, she had Margaret—but these cats were strange. They didn't come up to rub against your legs, they sat on their cushions and stared and winked, with glittery eyes just like the fortune-teller doll's. While Teddy was searching for his penny, she tried a tentative "Here kitty, kitty," but it didn't work. She tried to pet the one with only half an ear and it hissed at her.

"Hah!" Teddy shouted, and produced a penny. He stuck it into the slot. For a moment nothing happened. Then the whirring began again, this time with renewed vigor. The doll jerked its head back and forth and almost looked angry.

"The tide will turn, the tide will turn. Bring me some silver and I will tell your future."

A couple more whirs and jerks and the whole thing stopped with a loud squeak.

Martha and Teddy stared.

"Is that it?" Teddy asked the machine.

16

Oh, gosh, maybe he was hoping to hear something to make him feel better about his new life at the beach, Martha thought. It could be that Ted was just putting on an act about loving the hotel business.

"Forget it. It's just a way to get you to put in more money," Martha tried to comfort him. "You said yourself, you can't buy much for a penny."

"It was a dirty trick," Teddy said. He repeated it much louder. "Did you hear me? A dirty trick!"

"That thing can't hear you."

"Somebody's got to be around," Teddy said.

Martha noticed that there was a freshness in the air now, as if a window had been opened. Or a door. A definite breeze was coming down the hall, blowing away the unpleasant smell of cats.

Martha peeked out. The door was open! "Come on," she urged. "Before it locks again."

Without protest Teddy followed her. Once outside, they took deep breaths of the sea air. The sun was peeking through the clouds. It would be a nice day. With a sudden burst of joy Martha said, "Let's go down on the sand." As they walked on the hard sand, along the edge of the unfrozen waves, Martha felt herself minding the beach less.

"You know," Teddy said after a while, "that whole thing was pretty crazy."

"It was just a machine."

"Sure. But how come, when we were in the hall, it asked who was there and invited us in? And how come the door was locked and then suddenly open again?"

"Somebody was hiding somewhere, obviously. And the wind blew the stuck door open." The wind was certainly strong enough. It was whipping at Martha's scarf and turning her nose red.

"Maybe the place was haunted."

Martha shivered, but not from the idea of ghosts. She and Teddy were used to ghosts; they had already solved one case of a haunted house. "It's okay," she said. "I'm not grouchy anymore. You don't have to try to cheer me up."

Teddy removed his glasses to wipe off the spots of salt spray. "Who said I was trying to cheer you up?"

"Whatever," Martha said, hoping he would drop the subject. Now that she felt ungrumpy, she was determined to enjoy herself. She didn't need any ghosts on her mind.

But as they trudged back to the hotel, she looked up at the boardwalk. Something had caught her eye. Something exactly like a walking pile of dirty laundry, furtively keeping pace with them, darting in and out of the dark, shuttered doorways.

Martha blinked . . . and it was gone.

4.

When they got back to the hotel, Jemima was making a scene. She said her silver bracelet with the turquoise stones was missing from her room.

Mom was unsympathetic. "Look around, I'm sure you'll find it."

"I did look."

"Well, look again."

"Mommmm!" Jemima moaned.

Mom tried to shush her. "You know how you're always leaving your things everywhere. Just yesterday I found your rings on the bathroom sink. They could easily have fallen down the drain."

This made Jemima wail.

One of the guests, old Mr. Grayly, was coming slowly down the stairs. He stopped and gazed at Jemima with concern. "Can I be of help?"

"No, thank you," Mom told him. "My daughter's just lost a bracelet."

"I didn't lose it," Jemima piped up. "Somebody stole it."

"Oh, my," said Mr. Grayly.

"It has been *mislaid*," Mom said, giving Jemima a stern look, and when Mr. Grayly seemed unsure, she added, "Everything's fine."

"That's all right, then," Mr. Grayly said, and continued down the stairs.

"You can't go around accusing people of stealing," Mom whispered to Jemima when he had gone into the hotel sitting room.

"Stealing is a serious charge," Teddy said in a pompous way.

"Yes, Ted, we know," Mom said, sounding annoyed. "I'm sure Jemima will find her bracelet wherever she left it."

Jemima was furious. "You never believe me," she said, and sat down on the stair with a thud.

"I hope so," Teddy said, still being pompous. "We want to keep our guests happy."

"We're very happy here, Ted," Mom said. "Aren't we, Martha?"

Martha considered the question. She felt happier than she had this morning. Maybe a little happier than yesterday. But still, Christmas not going to be the same, and she wasn't happy about that.

Mom wasn't interested in hanging around for an answer anyway. She said she was hurrying out to meet Dad so they could finish up some Christmas shopping.

"Everything's closed," Martha called after her, but she was already out the door.

"There are stores open downtown," Teddy said. "There is civilization here, you know."

"They could at least have asked if I wanted to come," Jemima said, and sniffed.

"She's really upset about her bracelet," Teddy said to Martha. "Come on, let's help her look for it."

"You won't find it," Jemima said in a voice like doom.

"Well, it won't hurt to try," said Ted. "Was it a special bracelet?"

"My boyfriend gave it to me."

"He's not your boyfriend anymore," Martha reminded her.

"Still, it's a memento," said Teddy.

"Yeah," Jemima agreed.

Teddy pushed his glasses up his nose and scratched his head. "What we have to do is go backward in time. Think when you had the bracelet on last and then go over every step."

Jemima hesitated. "Oh, what the heck. I put it on my dresser before I went to bed, like I always do. It was there this morning, because I was going to put it on, but then I thought I'd take a jog on the beach before breakfast, so I didn't." She looked at them. "I mean, I wouldn't wear my good bracelet to go jogging, would I?" she asked, as if daring them to disagree.

"You had it on last night . . . and you put it on the dresser. . . ." Teddy began to mumble.

"We'd better get a paper and pencil for notes," Martha suggested.

"I'm making mental notes," Ted said. "You're sure about all this, Jemima?"

"Yes, I'm sure," Jemima said impatiently.

"Okay, okay. So you left it in your room while you had breakfast. When did you discover it was missing?"

Jemima rolled her eyes. "When I came back upstairs. And don't ask me if I'm sure, because I'm sure!"

Teddy pondered. "We had a full house this morning, and all the guests ate breakfast. Every one of them was in the dining room. I checked, you know, because we need to know how many breakfasts we serve and—"

"Not everyone," Martha interrupted.

"What do you mean?"

"We weren't in the dining room."

Teddy snorted. "You know what I mean, Martha. Nobody was upstairs at breakfast time."

"Well, I went up to brush my teeth, remember? And then other people must have gone up to their rooms too." Martha thought it was all getting pretty silly. "I mean, the guests didn't all march out together in a row, did they?"

"See! Anybody could have stolen it," Jemima exclaimed happily.

Teddy looked deflated. Martha decided to be more helpful.

"What we have to do is try to find out which guests went upstairs and which ones just went out," she said. "You were down here waiting for me, Ted. Did you notice?"

"I only noticed you come down," he replied. "But if you were upstairs, maybe you saw someone."

Martha thought. Of course, she'd heard that noise. And noticed the moldy velvet drape moving. She felt a little dopey for not remembering it sooner.

"I heard something when I was brushing my teeth. But I didn't see who it was."

"That's a big help," Jemima said.

"It's not my fault," Martha retorted. "I didn't know your bracelet was getting stolen, did I?"

"Let's not fight," Teddy said reasonably. "If we co-operate, we can get to the bottom of this."

"Oh, sure," said Jemima.

"What are you kids nattering about?" a voice asked. Petal Plum was coming down the staircase, her arms full of sheets and pillowcases.

Martha, Teddy, and Jemima all spoke at the same time.

"Nothing," said Martha.

"Nothing," said Teddy.

"My stolen bracelet," said Jemima.

Petal's eye got big and round. "Oooh," she said. "Who's the culprit?"

"We don't know yet," Jemima replied. "But these two are going to solve the crime." She smirked.

"I wouldn't go so far as to call it a crime yet," Teddy protested, looking nervous.

Petal nodded. "Innocent until proven guilty. Why don't you come into the kitchen for a snack and we'll talk it over."

"Any of those blueberry muffins left from yesterday?" Teddy asked, eagerly following Petal. Martha tagged along. Jemima stuck her fingers down inside the waistband of her jeans and frowned. "I'm getting fat," she muttered.

Petal told them to sit down at the table until she put the laundry into the washer. Then, as she served them milk and blueberry muffins, she asked them to tell her the whole story. Jemima started to speak but Teddy put up his hand. "Wait a minute. Petal, where's your mother?"

"At the market getting all the food for Christmas dinner."

"Okay, then. It's safe."

"What's my mother got to do with it?" Petal asked, suddenly suspicious.

Teddy's face got red. He sputtered and finally said, "Because she'll tell my mother."

Petal looked confused. "And so?"

"My mother will get mad," Teddy reluctantly replied.

Jemima brushed muffin crumbs off the front of her sweater. "Good. That makes two of us."

"No, you don't understand," Teddy said. "It's not good for business if things get stolen. We have to keep this quiet."

Jemima was amazed. "But what about my bracelet?" She got up from her chair. "I think we should call the police."

Teddy jumped up too. "No, no, you can't do that!"

Martha grabbed Jemima's arm before she could give Teddy a push.

"Calm down, all of you!" Petal bellowed. "Now, I've been thinking and I agree with Ted. You start screaming 'thief' and everyone will pack up and leave, and my poor old mum and me will be out of a job."

Jemima started to protest but Petal said, "Don't worry, we'll find out what's happened to your bracelet, but we'll do it very quietly, and with the help of an expert." Petal beamed around the table at them, her cheeks pinker than ever.

Jemima was unimpressed. "What expert?" She

pointed to Martha and Teddy. "You don't mean these two doodahs?"

"Of course not," Petal sniffed, and Martha felt herself bristle. What did Petal know about them, anyway? She and Teddy were experienced at solving things far more mysterious than a missing bracelet.

"We'll ask for the assistance of my fiancé," Petal was saying.

A boyfriend, Martha thought. Petal was as bad as Jemima.

"You mean Francis Hinkel?" Teddy asked.

"None other," Petal said proudly.

"So who's this Mr. Hinkel?" Jemima asked in a bored voice.

"*Officer* Hinkel," Petal corrected. "Upholder of the law." She leaned forward and whispered. "I'll ask him to go under cover for us."

"Really," Jemima said in an offhand way, but you could see she was suddenly interested.

"This is great," said Teddy, excitedly stuffing a big chunk of blueberry muffin into his mouth.

This is going too far, Martha thought with a sinking sensation. She wondered if this was what Petal had meant about moogly times. She certainly felt moogly, cooking up schemes involving undercover cops. Whatever it meant, it was as good a word as any for what she was feeling.

5.

Very early the next morning Teddy burst into Martha's room without knocking. Martha pulled the sheet up over her head, but Teddy pulled it down again.

"Get up quick," he cried.

Martha wondered if she had mixed up the days and it was Christmas morning and she was missing out on opening presents. Or maybe there had been an earthquake and the hotel was about to fall down. She pulled the sheet back up under her chin and glared. "Why?"

"It's happened." He ran to the window and threw it open. "Frozen waves!"

A gust of glacial air blew into the room, flapping the curtains and the pages of a magazine on the table beside the bed.

"Come and see," Teddy said.

Martha shivered and scrunched down under the blankets. "It's okay, I believe you. Close the window!"

Teddy obeyed, but not before he took a last look and pronounced, "I told you so.

"It's exactly the way Mrs. Plum said it would be; it looks like a ruffle, just like this." He came over to pull up a section of the frilly dust ruffle at the edge of Martha's bed.

"That's nice."

"Well, you're not very enthusiastic, are you?"

"I'm sorry, Ted. I really am. Maybe I'm getting a cold or something. I just can't get into a good mood."

"But I thought you were finished with the grouches yesterday, when we were planning our undercover operation."

"I thought so too. But there's just something funny about . . . I don't know . . . about everything." She sat up, not caring anymore if Teddy saw her panda pajamas. "Maybe it has to do with what Petal said. I felt funny yesterday, and this morning the waves are frozen. She warned that meant moogly times."

"She didn't explain, though, did she? Moogly times don't have to be bad. They could be really good times."

Martha sighed. "You're right. We'd better ask her."

"She went out early this morning," he said with concern. "Maybe she's having a rendezvous with Officer Hinkel."

"But I thought she saw him last night."

Petal had told them she would be meeting her fiancé after the dinner hour was over and the kitchen cleaned up. She called it "walking out" with him.

Teddy looked puzzled. "She said she would, but who knows, maybe he was on duty or something." Suddenly he was back into his hotel-business mode. "She'd better get back in time to serve breakfast or my mother will blow a fit."

Martha wondered about Teddy's mother. The impression Martha had was of a tall, blond, very busy lady who talked a lot, either on the phone or to her guests, but never to Martha. Once or twice she had given Martha a kind of businesslike smile. She wore very red lipstick, big gold earrings, and a lot of perfume. Martha hadn't been able to decide whether she was nice or not. And lately, all she'd heard was how mad she could get. She wasn't anything like Mom. Mom might speak sternly, but she wouldn't blow a fit. And she would stop what she was doing to listen if you had something serious on your mind. Mrs. Winterrab was always saying, "Not now, dear" or "Catch me later." Martha wondered what it would be like to have Mrs. Winterrab as a mother. She didn't seem very motherly.

"You're not listening," Teddy was saying, and Martha snapped back. "Get dressed as fast as you can so we can go down to the beach."

"Okay," Martha said. The room had warmed up again.

"I'll be in the dining room. I have to supervise until Petal gets back. She didn't even fold the napkins this morning, and some of the glasses had spots on them." He went out shaking his head, looking exactly like Martha's dad when he had business problems.

This made Martha giggle, and she got up and grabbed her plastic bag of bathroom supplies and ran down the hall.

Mr. Grayly was just coming out. His hair was all slicked with water and his face was red from shaving. He looked a little older and skinnier without his jacket on. Mr. Grayly always dressed up in a tie and jacket, even for breakfast.

"Good morning, Martha," he said.

"Good morning, Mr. Grayly," she replied, liking the sound of being so formal.

Mr. Grayly paused and Martha thought he was going to say something else, but he must have changed his mind because he went down the hall, walking very slowly and carefully.

The bathroom smelled of toothpaste and Mr. Grayly's shaving cream, and it was warm and steamy. Martha threw cold water on her face, combed her hair, and hurried back to her room to get dressed. As she passed Mr. Grayly's door, she noticed it was slightly ajar. An eye was intently peering through the crack between door and jamb. It was kind of creepy, as if Mr. Grayly was spying on her. But maybe he was just waiting to use the bathroom again, so she pretended not to notice.

When she got downstairs to the dining room, Teddy was pacing up and down, fretting over Petal's disappearance, and straightening a fork here or neatly folded napkin there.

Martha looked around at the small tables set with pink linen cloths, flowered china, and sparking glasses. "Everything looks fine, to me. Stop worrying, Ted."

He glanced anxiously at the big grandfather clock that stood between the windows. "They'll all be down soon, and Petal is supposed to start serving." Then his expression changed from worry to determination. "Come on, let's sneak out before Mrs. Plum makes us help. I'm not going to miss seeing those frozen waves."

It wasn't until they were walking over the dunes that

Martha remembered she hadn't been up in time to see if the raggedy creature had been on the beach again that morning. But Teddy must have been checking things out pretty early.

"So what time did you get up to see the waves?" she asked him.

"Almost before sunrise, like I've been doing every morning," he said smugly. "In the hotel business you have to get up very early."

"Yeah, well, I guess nobody else would want to be up at that hour. I don't suppose you ever see anybody out on the beach, not in the winter at least."

"No-oo . . ." Teddy said vaguely, and put his hand up to shield his eyes against the glare of the newly risen sun. "But there's somebody now. What a relief!"

Petal was trudging toward them. She raised a bare hand in greeting. She was wearing big green Wellington boots and had a scarf looped loosely around her throat. Her nose was red, with a frozen drop of sniffle hanging off the end, but she didn't look the least bit chilly.

"Where have you been, Petal?" Teddy said peevishly.

"Having a look at this." She gestured toward the water, and Martha really noticed for the first time how the waves seemed as if they were suspended in time, caught in the moment of crashing against the shore. Ice crystals glinted red, blue, and violet in the sun.

Martha now understood why Teddy had been so anxious to see the frozen waves. She suddenly felt happy to be standing on a beach in the middle of winter. "It's beautiful," she said to Petal.

Petal shook her head. "Moogly is what it is."

"Is that something really bad?" Martha asked.

"It's going to be really bad if you don't get up to the hotel and start serving breakfast," Teddy interrupted.

Petal looked at her watch and gave out a screech like a banshee. "I've lost complete track of the time!"

"You certainly have," Teddy began. Martha could see he was pumping himself up to make one of his pompous speeches. She wondered if the kids at the school here knew he used to be called Teddy Windbag because he talked so much.

But Petal wasn't listening. She was thumping over the hard sand in her big boots, her red hair flying out like fire all over her head.

"Let's go too," Martha said. "All this fresh air has made me hungry."

"We'll wait a few minutes," Ted said, watching Petal disappear into the kitchen door, "to make sure the coast is clear."

"Gosh, Teddy, is your mother that awful?" As soon as she asked the question, Martha wished she could take it back. It wasn't the kind of question you should ask your friend about his mother.

But Teddy acted as if he hadn't heard. Finally Martha had to yank his arm to get him moving. "Come on," she said, "or you'll freeze solid, just like your famous waves."

6.

Mrs. Plum was good at doing lots of things at once. When Martha and Teddy came into the kitchen, she was stirring oatmeal, poaching eggs, frying up sausages, toasting thick slices of bread, and keeping an eye on the Christmas pudding that was boiling away in a big pot. Martha had never seen a pudding being boiled before. Mrs. Plum explained.

"It's traditional, lovey. Full of raisins, nuts, candied fruit, and plums, because it's a plum pudding, ha ha. It has to boil for five hours and then sit for a day or two to get nice and mature. I'll serve it at Christmas dinner with hard sauce."

Martha wondered how a sauce could be hard.

"In my family in the old days we had lovely Christmases," Mrs. Plum mused, spooning big dollops of oatmeal into their bowls. "So many people. My grandma had to use five pounds of flour for some of her cakes. And always a nice roast goose."

Martha wondered how a goose would taste. Like turkey, maybe. She knew they were having roast turkey for the Belleflower Christmas dinner. A gala dinner with all the trimmings, Mrs. Winterrab had told them in her Christmas special invitation. That was one of the reasons Mom had wanted to come. No cooking, she'd said happily.

Mrs. Plum kept on talking about the past as she bustled around the kitchen, stopping only to give orders to Petal, who was serving the breakfasts speedily but looking a little disheveled. Teddy checked to make sure she had taken off her boots.

"I wish it would snow on Christmas Day," he said, pouring cream onto his oatmeal. "That would be traditional."

Mrs. Plum gave him a sharp look. "Always wishing for something! You'll wish your life away if you don't watch out."

Martha agreed. It was typical. No sooner had Teddy seen his frozen waves than he was on another kick. Now he'd be up every morning at dawn checking for snow. She didn't think she could stand it.

"Nothing wrong with wishes," Teddy said. "As long as they're good ones. I think maybe it helps good things to happen if you wish for them."

Mrs. Plum looked skeptical. "Good things happen if you deserve them," she said firmly.

"Well, there's nothing wrong with a little snow," Teddy persisted.

"I'll bet your mother can find plenty wrong with it," Mrs. Plum said. "She's got those extra people figured in for the holiday meals. If the roads are bad, they won't come and we'll be stuck with mounds of food."

Teddy immediately got serious. "I never thought of that!" he exclaimed. "I'll change my wish. No snow, no snow!"

Mrs. Plum laughed and went back to tossing sausages around in the black iron frying pan. "You'll have to take whatever happens."

Teddy pondered. "Yeah, but wouldn't it be great for the hotel business if you could see the future?"

"Nobody can do that, although plenty try," said Mrs. Plum. She put the frying pan down. "Now, there's something I'd forgotten all about. There used to be a fortune-teller in this town and she predicted the future right every time."

"Is she still around?" Teddy asked eagerly.

"Well, it wasn't exactly a person," Mrs. Plum said. "It was a sort of mechanical doll. I'm sure there was a person behind the scenes, but everybody wanted to believe in the doll. There's a seafood restaurant where the old shop used to be. It's been gone a long time now."

Martha and Teddy looked at each other. "But we've seen her," Teddy said.

"Seen who, lovey?" Mrs. Plum asked, distracted with the sausages that had started to burn.

"The fortune-telling doll. We saw her yesterday on the boardwalk."

"Boardwalk's all shut up for the winter," said Mrs. Plum.

"One place was open," Martha said. "And we saw a doll that told fortunes. If you put in a penny first."

Mrs. Plum looked astonished. "That sounds just like it," she said. "How did it go? 'Put in your penny and your fortune I shall tell.' "

"Yeah, that's right. Except now it just tells you to come back with quarters," Teddy said.

"But who on earth is doing business on the board-walk at this time of year?"

"Somebody with a lot of smelly cats," said Martha.

"Well, don't you two start getting ideas," Mrs. Plum warned. "It was all stuff and nonsense when I was a child, and it won't be any different now."

Teddy was disappointed. "But you said the doll really told the future."

"I didn't say I believed it," said Mrs. Plum. "And you shouldn't either."

"Either it tells the future or it doesn't," Teddy protested. "It's easy enough to prove one way or the other."

Mrs. Plum's jolly face turned dour. "Not another word about it."

Teddy clammed up, but Martha knew he was still thinking. It would be just like him to want to go back and ask the doll to tell him the road conditions for Christmas Day. What a waste. If you could really find out the future, there were all sorts of better things to ask about. Like whether she was getting the gold locket she'd asked for. She could even ask if Mellow would make up with Jemima. She suspected Jemima was just pretending that she didn't care. A couple of times Martha caught her checking the mail in a sneaky way. Probably to see if Mellow had sent a card. And her ears always pricked up when the telephone rang. Martha sat there, having a nice think about all the possibilities. Like what Dad could ask about his business prospects and not have to worry so much. And . . .

"Are you finished?" Teddy was asking, and before

she could answer he had snatched away her bowl and spoon.

"What's the big rush?"

"We have things to do," he said. And when he noticed Mrs. Plum giving him a look he added in a loud voice, "You know, we have to finish our Christmas shopping."

Martha started to say she had used up all her allowance, but Teddy gave her leg a kick.

"Thanks for the nice breakfast, Mrs. Plum," Martha said, and followed Teddy out of the kitchen and into the front hall.

"Sometimes you sure are slow," Teddy said. "We've got to get back over to that fortune-teller right away."

"Well," Martha said, "okay. But, I mean, do we have to exactly run out the door this minute?"

"Of course we do," he replied. "Some guests are checking out today. If we hurry, we can ask about Jemima's bracelet and make sure the thief doesn't get away!"

"Mrs. Plum didn't say anything about questions like that," Martha told him as she struggled into her jacket and squashed her wool hat down on her head. "She only said it could tell the future."

"We'll think of the right wording as we walk over," Teddy said, undaunted. "There's got to be a way."

"I guess we won't need the services of Officer Hinkel after all," Martha puffed. "Petal will be disappointed."

"See, your brain is slow as molasses these days," Teddy said in dismay. "Of *course* we'll need Officer Hinkel. Who else is going to arrest the thief?"

It must be the sea air, Martha thought. It kept re-minding her of summer vacations. Her brain thought she should be lazing around, thinking about taking another dip in the ocean or having another lemonade. Instead she was chugging along in the freezing cold, on her way to solving a crime.

7.

The door with the knocker in the shape of a bird was firmly locked. Nobody answered their knocks. Teddy gave it a kick just for good measure. Nothing would budge it.

"Never mind," Martha said. "If we hang around long enough, someone will be back."

"I'm not so sure. This door looks like it hasn't been opened in a hundred years. We didn't dream it, did we?"

"Of course not. Someone *has* to come back to take care of those cats." At least she hoped so. They had looked awfully skinny and the place had smelled bad. It would be terrible if the cats were trapped inside. There were probably lots of mice to eat, but what about water?

"Maybe they weren't really cats," Teddy said.

"What are you talking about? We saw them; we certainly smelled them. They were cats."

"I mean, maybe they were something else in the shape of cats."

Martha shivered, but she told herself it was because of the icy wind, not because she was getting a case of the creeps. "Don't be silly."

Teddy suddenly brightened up. "I know what we can do. We can ask Officer Hinkel for a search warrant."

Martha was a little skeptical, but it might be worth a try. They could use the cats as an excuse. People were always concerned about the rights of animals. They would keep their mouths shut about fortune-tellers and say they needed the door opened for humane reasons. Yeah, it was a good idea, she told Teddy. "Let's go back and ask Petal where to find him."

"I think I know where he is," Teddy said. "It will save time."

They hurried through the narrow streets of closed shops and came out onto a big avenue. It was like discovering civilization after being lost in the desert. Stores were open, people were shopping, Christmas trees were for sale on the corner, and cars zoomed up and down. In the center of the intersection, directing traffic, was a tall man in a uniform.

"Hey, Francis!" Teddy yelled across to him.

Martha was shocked. It didn't seem the proper way to address a police officer.

Officer Hinkel didn't seem to mind. He signaled for them to wait, and then, after he had pushed something in a box on the traffic light, he came over. Teddy introduced him to Martha. She had to crane her neck to get a look at his face, he was so tall. He had the bluest eyes Martha had ever seen.

Before Martha could even say how do you do, Teddy plunged right in. "We need a search warrant fast!"

"We do, huh?" Officer Hinkel said. Martha could

tell he thought Teddy was just being harebrained. She pinched Teddy's arm to signal him to shut up.

"We're concerned about some abandoned cats," Martha said. That didn't sound much better.

"I thought Petal told you all about it," Teddy tried again.

Officer Hinkel rocked back on his heels and considered. "Petal told me about a missing bracelet. She didn't say anything about abandoned cats."

"Believe me, they're connected," Teddy said, "only it would take too long to explain how. What we really need to do is get inside this locked-up place on the boardwalk." He caught Martha's eye. "Er . . . to save these cats."

"Cats make me sneeze," Officer Hinkel said. "But I don't wish them any harm. Merchants use them to keep down the mice. Are you sure they're abandoned?"

"These are really thin cats," Teddy said earnestly.

"Mice all went south for the winter, I guess," said Officer Hinkel with a bright smile full of white teeth.

"You're not taking us seriously," Teddy complained in a whiny voice, but Officer Hinkel took no notice. He told them to contact the ASPCA about the cats, and he said they could also stop by police headquarters to make a report. Martha thought he seemed genuinely concerned about the cats, considering he was allergic to them.

"That's *it*?" Teddy asked.

"That's the procedure for a start," Officer Hinkel replied.

"Well, it's not going to get us anywhere," Teddy

41

started to complain. Martha firmly took Ted's arm and thanked Officer Hinkel for his help.

"Anytime," he said, with a salute. "But watch yourselves on the boardwalk. There are some odd sorts camping there in winter. Fly-by-night people, here one day, gone the next."

"We'll be careful," Martha said politely, since Teddy just kept on muttering complaints under his breath.

"Oh, by the way," Officer Hinkel said as he went back to direct traffic, "tell Petal I haven't forgotten what she told me. Tell her I'll be coming around to talk it over."

"What?" Teddy gasped. Martha pulled him away. "Thanks again," she called to Officer Hinkel.

"But, Martha, did you hear what he said? If he comes to the hotel and starts interrogating the guests, it will be a disaster. We've got to stop him."

"We'll be arrested for obstructing justice," Martha said, keeping a firm grip on Ted's arm.

"Where are you taking me? Stop a minute, will you? You're going in the wrong direction."

"I just wanted to get you away from that policeman before you made a fool of yourself."

She let him go and he made a show of brushing himself off and regaining his composure. "That Petal's a traitor," he said after a moment.

"You don't think she took Jemima's bracelet?"

"No, I mean she just humored us, because we're kids. She said she'd get Francis to go under cover and keep the robbery quiet and instead she just went and reported it to him in the regular way."

Martha thought a moment. "That can't be true. She

really wanted to keep it quiet. Remember? She was worried about her job."

"I don't trust her anymore."

"Look, we don't have to give up. Let's give it another try. Maybe there's a back door to that fortune-telling place."

Teddy perked up. "Good idea. And on our way we'll stop at the market for a can of cat food."

"That's nice, Ted, but one can won't be enough."

"One can is all we need," he said mysteriously. "I have my reasons, you'll see."

8.

They bought the can of cat food at the market. Teddy insisted on asking which one smelled the best to cats. The manager said how would he know, he wasn't a cat. But a lady who was shopping with her children was glad to make a recommendation. She said she had three cats and they absolutely loved the one with fish chunks.

Teddy thanked her, read the label, made a gaggy face, and charged it to his mother's hotel account. He also charged a can opener. Then they hurried over to the boardwalk.

Just to be sure, they tried the door again, knocking hard to see if anyone was inside.

"Okay, we go for the back door," Teddy said.

It was a long walk to the end of the boardwalk, before they could get to the backs of the stalls and arcades. There were a lot of windows and doors and basement entrances, some overgrown with weeds and dune grass or half covered with sandy soil. It was hard to figure out which was the rear of the fortune-teller's shop.

"I guess my idea wasn't so hot," Martha said.

Teddy held up the cat food. "That's why I brought this."

He made a quick guess at the general location and proceeded to open the can. Then he walked around holding the can out and saying, "Here, kitty, kitty."

After only a few minutes a bunch of skinny, mean-looking cats came scrambling out of an opening in one of the lower windows.

"There they are!" Teddy said.

"Gosh, that was a good idea," Martha told him, impressed.

"Only because your idea was not to give up. We do best when we work as a team, Marth. But until now we didn't seem to be doing too well."

"I know. I guess it was my grumpy mood. Anyhow, that window seems to be unlocked, and those cats are the same ones we saw inside yesterday." Martha recognized the one with half an ear and another long orange one that was now trying to crawl up Teddy's leg.

"Wait a minute until I put this can down." The cats were clawing around his ankles, mewling like crazy. "I hope we haven't started a riot."

He dumped the cat food out onto the pavement and the cats swarmed around. It proved Martha's worst fear: the cats were neglected, probably starving.

The window, grimy and impossible to see through, resisted at first when Teddy pushed at it. Then it went up with a grinding squeak. They peered in at a gloomy cellar.

Teddy looked at Martha. "Yes or no?"

She sniffed at the dank air. There were a lot of cobwebs around the window, but the cellar looked pretty ordinary. She could see a staircase going to the upper floor and the door at the top was open. "Officer Hinkel would call this trespassing," she said.

"It's for a good cause. We're liberating the cats. Look at them, they're all running off now that they have the strength. It's only fair to check to see if more are being held captive inside."

"All right, I'm convinced."

They crawled through.

There was nothing scary about the cellar. It was full of old stuff: books, posters, framed pictures of peculiar people, and a whole trunkful of old-fashioned clothes. Martha took a quick peek and discovered a nest of baby mice in a feather boa. Good thing they hadn't been eaten! She hoped the cats would never come back.

Teddy told her to come with him up the stairs. "I want to have a crack at that fortune-telling doll before anybody catches us," he said. Martha had almost forgotten why they'd come. She wished she could just stay and explore the cellar.

"I wasn't counting on getting caught," she whispered to him. "Keep your voice down."

Teddy nodded and they went slowly up the stairs, watching for creaks. At the top they stopped to listen. "I think the coast is clear," Ted said.

The place seemed even more desolate and dirty than it had the day before. The fortune-telling doll was in her case, the only bright thing in the room. Her black eyes seemed to glitter with recognition when they slunk in. But of course that was only a trick of the light. There were no more cats.

Teddy was suddenly flustered. "I hope I have

enough money," he said, jamming his hands into his pockets. "No sense bothering with pennies. We'll go for the big time with a dime. That counts as silver, doesn't it?"

"I don't know if they make them out of silver anymore, but the principle is the same."

Teddy stuck a dime into the slot. Nothing happened. He tried another dime. Nothing. He stuck in a nickel. It fell out again. "Okay, okay," he said to the motionless doll. "I'm doing my best. Martha, have you got any quarters?"

Martha had exactly one quarter to her name. She'd spent all her money on Christmas gifts and allowance wasn't until next week. She didn't really want to give it up. She was saving it for some emergency, if you could deal with an emergency for a quarter. Well, she supposed this was one.

"You could have planned ahead a little," she couldn't help saying.

It was a total waste of a quarter. The doll stood in her case, looking evil but useless. Teddy tried his question anyway.

"Look, maybe you're not in the mood but since we put in the silver like you wanted, could you please just answer one question? It's no big deal, probably, but it would save a lot of trouble at my mother's hotel. The question is: Who took Jemima's bracelet?"

"You were going to reword it," Martha reminded him. "She can only tell you the future, remember?"

Teddy looked aggravated, but he tried again. "How's this: Will the thief who stole Jemima's bracelet be leaving tomorrow?"

48

The doll gave him a blank stare back.

Teddy was furious, and Martha wasn't exactly happy to have spent her quarter for nothing. Then she spied a lever labeled COIN RETURN. She gave it a push and the coins came jingling down a chute and fell onto the floor.

"Wow!" Teddy said, doing a rapid calculation. There were at least five quarters in addition to his two dimes.

"It's not all ours," Martha said, hating herself for sounding like such a goody-goody. But she didn't want to take anything from the fortune-teller. She had a feeling it would be bad luck. In fact, the place was beginning to make her nervous. They had no business being here at all. She could just see herself arrested and thrown into jail. What a way to spend Christmas.

They stood there for a moment, staring at the doll. It was crazy, but Martha thought she heard the faintest beginnings of a whir. And then there was the unmistakable sound of a key being put into a lock on the front door. Someone was coming!

They read each other's minds and, wordlessly, made for the cellar stairs. They got down them just as footsteps could be heard overhead. There wasn't time to be sure they were safe enough to wiggle back through the window, so they dived behind the big trunk of old clothes and crouched there, listening to the footsteps and the low muttering of voices.

More clothes were strewn behind the trunk, but Martha had lost all interest in the stuff. All she could think of was getting out of there without being caught.

She kept her eyes glued on the cellar steps, praying that whoever had come in would stay upstairs.

She heard a sharp intake of breath beside her and a strange gurgling sound. Her first thought was that Teddy had been nabbed and was being strangled. But when she looked, it was Teddy strangling himself, covering his mouth so he wouldn't give them away by crying out. He pointed at the strewn clothes under their feet.

"Kids' clothes," he mouthed when she had shrugged her shoulders and shaken her head to indicate she didn't understand. "Not old. Look." He held up a threadbare and stained, but obviously modern, T-shirt and a pair of boy's Fruit of the Loom underpants.

Martha didn't know why he was so interested in a bunch of dirty clothes. It was more important to be thinking about getting out of there.

There was a sudden terrible shriek from above. "My babies, my babies!" a distraught voice cried. Like the skinny cats, Martha and Teddy were out that cellar window in a flash and running from the fortune-teller's shop like it was poison. They didn't stop until they were in sight of the hotel.

"What was that all about back there?" Martha asked, bending over because she had a stitch in her side.

"Clothes . . . just left there without anyone in them," Teddy panted. "I told you those cats weren't cats. I bet that fortune-teller is a kidnapper and a witch."

Martha gawked at him.

"She changed them, don't you see? She got these

kids into her shop and she turned them all into cats! Did you hear her scream when she realized they were gone? We were dead meat. It's a lucky thing we escaped."

"You'd better not mention this to anyone else," Martha said.

"Of course not, they wouldn't believe us."

"Right."

Teddy looked at her. "Do I get the feeling *you* don't believe me?"

Martha hedged. "I'm not saying it's impossible. But I'm not exactly saying it's possible either."

Teddy was indignant. "We talked to a real live spirit once, didn't we? And to a ghost in a haunted house? What's so hard about believing this?"

Martha thought about the cats, all shapes and sizes, all different colors, some with long hair, some with short. She tried to imagine them, skinny and nasty as they had been, as kids. She had to giggle.

"Okay, forget I said anything." Teddy walked off in a huff. Martha followed, realizing they'd missed lunch. She wondered if Mrs. Winterrab would throw a fit.

9.

A big ruckus was waiting for them when they got back late for lunch. Everybody had been worried and on the verge of calling the police. It was Mrs. Plum who had said to wait just a little longer and who calmed everyone down. But it was Mrs. Plum who was really the maddest. When Mrs. Winterrab saw that Teddy was home safe, she went back to her office to do the hotel books, saying, "Next time you decide to take off all day, at least leave word at the desk!" Martha thought she made Teddy sound more like a hotel guest than her own son.

Actually, what Mom and Dad said to Martha was almost the same thing, but somehow it came out differently and sounded nicer.

"It only takes a minute to let us know," Dad told her calmly.

"We worry about you because we love you," said Mom.

Jemima told Martha she was a major pain. "They expected me to go out and run around town looking for you," she said. "I mean, really."

"Thanks a lot," Martha said.

"Oh, well, I guess I would've," Jemima said. "You

came back in the nick of time. I want to wash my hair. You know the afternoon's the only time nobody else wants to get into the bathroom."

Mrs. Plum gave them what she called a couple of pieces of her mind. She sat them down at the kitchen table.

"Don't think I don't know what you've been up to, because I do. It took all my wits to keep them from sounding the alarm. They thought you'd drowned or worse. But I knew you went slinking over to that mechanical fortune-telling monster you told me you'd seen." She folded her arms over her chest and peered at them. "You did, didn't you?"

Martha wasn't sure Mrs. Plum really expected an answer. Neither she nor Teddy gave one, but Mrs. Plum said, "There, I knew it!" just as if they'd said yes.

"More than one fool has been parted from his money messing about with fortune-tellers. Keep your money in your pocket and the future will take care of itself," Mrs. Plum advised. "And never ever go off without telling your mother again," she said to Ted. Then she looked at Martha. "The same for you, young lady."

"Yes, ma'am," Teddy said.

"Yes, Mrs. Plum."

"That's better." She opened the oven and took out the two plates she'd kept warm for them.

"But we might have drowned or whatever's worse," Teddy said. "How could you be so sure?"

Mrs. Plum sealed up her mouth into a tight line, but she couldn't keep a small smile from fluttering at her lips. "I have my methods," she said. "Maybe I can tell fortunes too."

Mrs. Plum went off to do some of the hotel house-keeping, leaving them alone in the kitchen.

"Do you think she was following us?" Martha asked Ted.

"No way. I know what happened. The market called to ask about the charges. And then Petal probably talked to Francis and he told her about the cats. Mrs. Plum just put two and two together. But don't say anything. She likes to think she has mystical powers."

"Then why should she care if we visit some stupid fortune-teller doll?"

"Who knows why adults act the way they do?"

After lunch Martha went up to her parents' room to help Dad wrap the gifts he'd bought for Mom and Jemima. It was his idea that they should have some quiet time together after all the excitement.

"We haven't seen much of each other since we arrived here," he said.

"I guess not. But aren't you and Mom having fun?"

Dad smiled. "It's our first vacation in quite a few years. It takes some getting used to."

"You mean, doing nothing but relaxing can make you feel weird, right?"

Dad seemed surprised that Martha knew how he felt. She told him how she'd thought the same thing, not having to do any chores. "Maybe they should have hotels where you help with the cooking and cleaning," she said.

Dad laughed. "I don't think Mom would think that arrangement was worth paying for."

"I was sort of disappointed when I got here," Martha confessed. "But I think I'm glad now." She almost wanted to tell him everything she and Ted had done that morning, but she thought she'd better not. Dad wouldn't think it was so great for them to be sneaking into strange cellars. It would scare him too much.

"I don't think Teddy's very happy, though," Martha said as she helped Dad tie a red bow on one of the boxes.

"Why not?"

"He's not like his old self anymore. And, well, I hope it's okay to say it, but his mother doesn't seem to like him very much."

"Now, Marth, I'm sure she loves him."

"Well, maybe I meant *interested.* She doesn't seem very interested in him."

Dad was silent for a while. Martha knew he was thinking about what she'd said. It wasn't like Dad to gossip about adults to her or Jemima. But she could tell that Dad sort of agreed with her, just like they'd agreed about the problems of relaxing.

"It's a little harder for Mrs. Winterrab," he said at last. "She doesn't have Teddy's father around to help."

"Lots of kids at school have single parents," Martha said. "But they always try to do stuff with their kids and come to the school activities. Mrs. Winterrab hardly ever did. She used to leave Teddy all alone for a whole weekend!"

Dad looked a little disapproving, and Martha knew he wasn't going to get into a big discussion about whether Mrs. Winterrab was a good mother or not. Instead he said, "You can't go around fixing people's problems, Martha. They have to work them through in their own way."

Martha smiled. "You mean we can't adopt Teddy and take him home, right?"

Dad looked horrified. "Good heavens, no!"

"Don't worry, I wouldn't be able to stand it either."

They wrapped all the gifts and put them away in a shopping bag so Mom and Jemima wouldn't be tempted to snoop. Martha would have liked to snoop at her own presents, but she was sure Dad had hidden them good.

Dad said he was going to take a nap. "There's Christmas caroling tonight, from house to house. And then tomorrow's the big tree-trimming party. There's plenty on the agenda."

Martha said she'd go down and find Teddy and she promised they wouldn't get into more trouble. "We'll play a boring old board game, Dad."

"Good," he said. "We don't want you getting lost. It would spoil Christmas, wouldn't it?"

Martha suddenly thought of the cats. Where had they gone? Were they out, wandering around, lost?

"Dad?"

"Yes, Marth?" he asked sleepily.

"There's no such thing as witches, right?"

Dad thought she was kidding around. He laughed and told her not to read too many fairy tales.

She shut the door quietly and went downstairs to

find Teddy. They wouldn't be able to play board games. They'd have to go out to round up those cats and return them to the person at the fortune-teller shop. Whoever she was, she had sounded very upset when she saw they were gone, as upset as Mom and Dad would be if Martha got lost. She'd have a lousy rotten Christmas if her cats never came back.

Teddy was in the hotel parlor, watching a soap on TV.

"Listen, we've done a terrible thing," Martha said.

"Shhhh, I can't hear. I think Gloria is going to tell Diane that Barbara murdered Pete."

"Shut that junk off," Martha ordered. "And listen to me. We have a job to do. We have to undo what we've done."

"You're talking just like a soap opera."

"Go and leave word at the desk," Martha directed. "And let's get cracking."

10.

They charged two more cans of cat food at the market and went back to the rear of the fortune-teller's shop. The cats might not have gone far, and it was the only place they could think of to start anyway.

Teddy opened one of the cans and they began to creep around saying, "Here, kitty, kitty," very quietly, just in case the fortune-teller people could hear them. But except for a very fat cat with a fancy velvet-and-rhinestone collar that came out of one of the nearby houses, there were no takers.

"Should we give him some?" Teddy asked, looking down at the sleekly groomed gray-and-white cat.

"Don't waste our supplies. We have a lot of territory to cover."

They widened their circles. The fat cat followed patiently behind Teddy, keeping a beady eye on the fish-chunk cat food.

Finally, Teddy just sat down on the ground. "This is no good. We can't go around the entire town saying, 'Here, kitty, kitty.' It will be like the Pied Piper of Hamelin. The whole cat population will be following us, like him here."

The fat cat stopped licking away at the top of the cat food to look up and twitch a whisker.

Martha sat down too. "You're right. And we'd never know who was who anyway. I can only identify one or two of them. How about you?"

"You're way ahead of me. One cat looks like another cat to me, except maybe for this snob. I prefer dogs."

Teddy's face clouded at this thought of dogs, and he grew more morose. It was cold sitting on the ground, and a wet sort of wind had come up. Bleak clouds scudded across an iron-gray sky. Martha felt like going back to the hotel and asking Mrs. Plum to make her a cup of hot cocoa. But she also felt responsible.

"The least we can do is check that window to see if it's still open. I'll feel better if I know the cats can get in if they come back by themselves."

"For all we know, they're already in."

"You could be right! I wish we knew one way or the other."

Teddy heaved himself to his feet. "Let's look at the window. Then let's go home."

He left the can of cat food for the fancy cat. "Merry Christmas," he said.

They sneaked up to the window, even though it didn't look like anyone was watching. Teddy looked it over carefully, gave it a tentative push, and said, "It's locked."

"How can it be? We left it open."

"It's locked now. Somebody probably came down to the cellar looking for the cats and saw how they had escaped."

"Oh, dear," Martha said. "The poor little things."

"They were a mean bunch, you said so yourself. Anyway, aren't you glad they've been liberated? I thought the whole idea was to rescue them from that creepy place where they were being held captive and starved to death."

"Oh, shut up. I've changed my mind about all that."

Teddy paid no attention. "And what about giving some consideration to *my* theory instead of just expounding on your own? What about all those lost or kidnapped kids that have been changed into mean and skinny cats?"

"What about it?"

Teddy stopped short. "What do you mean, what about it?"

"You asked the question. So okay, what about your theory? If the cats are really bewitched, how can we help them change back into kids if they're running all over town being cats?"

"I never thought of that. We really do need to find them, don't we?"

"Or find out if they've already come back. You know, they might have looked scruffy, but that woman called them her babies. I think she really loved them. What if they had a little run and returned home while we were back at the hotel? She'd leave the window open if they weren't back. But I'm sure she'd lock it so they couldn't get out again."

A big snowflake plunked down on Teddy's nose. Then another and another. "I think that's an excellent theory, Martha. Forget mine and let's get out of here."

"No, I can't. I simply have to know or I won't enjoy Christmas."

Teddy's face scrinched up against the wet snow. "But what can we do? Go around and knock on the door and say, 'It's five o'clock, do you know where your cats are?'"

Martha gave him the benefit of a small laugh. "If we asked that, she'd know we had something to do with their getting out. She might put a hex on us."

"I thought you didn't go for my witch theory."

"I don't. But it doesn't hurt to take precautions."

"Well, we better think of something fast. I'm freezing and we'll be late for the caroling and I don't want another big fuss from my mother."

Martha felt abashed. Here she was worrying about some cats she didn't even know personally when her best friend was having problems with his mother. Talk about lost kids. Poor Teddy could be one of them, the way things with his mother were going.

"All right," she said, resigned to giving up on the cats. "Let's go. But I don't think I'm gonna feel much like singing."

"You'll get in the mood once it starts. It's one of the best parts of Christmas."

Martha stopped in her tracks. "That's it!"

"What?"

"Singing. Carols. We go around and knock on the door and we sing a carol. And while we're singing, we sneak looks to see if the cats are inside."

"I'm not singing any carols to some daft old witch. What about the hex?"

"She won't suspect anything. Everybody will be out singing today."

"She'll wonder why it's only two of us."

"She'll think we're cute."

Teddy gave her a long, hard look. "You know,

Martha, sometimes . . ." he began. "Oh, okay, I'll do it. But only because you're my friend and because it's Christmas. Count it as part of your Christmas present."

They wiped their noses and Teddy remembered to stuff the unopened can of cat food down in his parka pocket. They decided they'd sing "We Wish You a Merry Christmas," because they both knew the tune and all the words. Then, taking a deep breath for courage and voice, they climbed up on the boardwalk and knocked on the wooden door. Unlike before, this time the door opened promptly. A woman stood there staring at them, looking alarmed and disappointed, as if she'd been expecting someone else.

"Whatta you want?"

Martha and Teddy stared back. She wasn't at all like a traditional witch. She was a short, square-shaped woman with a lot of muscles in her arms. They could see them because she was wearing some kind of elastic outfit that had no sleeves. Her hair was pulled up on top of her head in an overflowing grayish-blond topknot. There was a cigarette hanging out the corner of her bright orange mouth.

"I asked whatta you want?"

Martha grabbed Teddy's hand, sounded the first note, and they launched into the carol.

"We wish you a merry Christmas, we wish you a merry Christmas, we wish you a merry Christmas and a happy New Year. . . . We wish you a—"

"That's nice, but that's enough," the woman said, starting to close the door. Teddy began to sing louder and Martha tried a little harmony.

The woman took the cigarette out of her mouth, sprinkled ashes at their feet, and looked nervously up and down the street. "Look, I mean it, kids—it's real nice but I can't afford to be standing out here."

Martha was singing and trying to see into the dim interior of the hall. If she could just get a look at only one cat, she wouldn't feel so bad.

She noticed that Teddy had slowly edged closer and had one foot stuck over the threshold. She also noticed that there was a big gob of chunky fish cat food stuck to one of his shoes and another gob on his parka sleeve.

And, as if at that precise moment they had noticed these things, too, a pack of skinny, mean-looking cats came running from around and between the woman's legs, and began mewling, groveling, and chewing at Teddy's feet.

"No, you don't, not again," the woman growled at the cats. Deftly, she scooped them up in handfuls and threw them back down the hall. Martha was horrified. She began to protest. But Teddy clamped a hand over her mouth.

"Merry Christmas to all and to all a good night!" he shouted, and urged Martha down the boardwalk as fast as they could walk without making it look like running.

11.

Martha considered saying she was too tired to go out caroling. It wasn't a lie. She had been back and forth to the boardwalk all day and just felt like crawling into bed. But Dad and Mom got all dressed up, with red scarves around their necks and glittery bits of pine and holly pinned on their lapels. They expected her to be as excited as they were, so Martha reluctantly changed into her red wool sweater. Mom combed her hair and tied it with another red ribbon. "We're all ready," she said, looking at their reflections in the mirror. "Now, where's Jemima?"

"She was in the bathroom, last I knew," Dad said.

Mom couldn't believe it. "But she's been in there practically all afternoon!" She marched down the hall and rapped on the bathroom door. "Jemima! Everyone's ready!"

"You go ahead. Don't worry about me, I'll catch up."

"The idea is to all start out *together*, dear," Mom explained. "It's time to come downstairs to collect your candle and carol book."

"I can't."

"What's wrong? Are you sick?"

"No, I'm fine."

Mom sighed. "Then why can't you come out, dear?" she asked patiently, the way she might ask a two-year-old.

"I just can't."

Dad intervened. "Jemima, that's not good enough. Now, open the door and speak to your mother properly."

"But my hair's a mess."

Dad looked angry. Mom said, "You'll be wearing a hat, dear. Nobody will notice your hair."

There was a terrible groan and the door opened slowly to reveal Jemima. Her hair was a lurid mixture of red and green stripes, sticking out all over her head.

Mom said something that sounded exactly like *eeeek* and grabbed Dad's arm. Dad's mouth hung open. Martha got over the shock quicker and began to laugh.

"Oh, shut up!" Jemima wailed. Martha tried to stop.

"What on earth did you do?" Mom asked.

Jemima held up a packet of hair dye. "It was supposed to give me fun streaks in Christmas colors," she said. "Easy to use and easy to wash out. It says so on the box." Her lip quivered and big tears rolled down her cheeks. "I'm ruined forever!"

"Maybe she can sue them, Dad," Martha suggested, and started laughing again.

"Stick your hat on your head and let's go," Mom ordered. "There's no time to do anything now."

"You're a big help," Jemima snarled at Martha as they went down the stairs.

"Sorry," Martha said, and made a supreme effort to

stop smiling. "But look at the bright side. At least Mellow's not here to see you."

"Yeah, you're right. This hotel is full of old fogeys." She tugged at the wool cap. "Are you sure nothing shows?"

"Not a thing."

The guests had assembled in the front hall, all of them decorated like Christmas trees. Petal was there, too, wearing a bright green beret over her red hair, creating just the effect Jemima had wanted. Martha looked around nervously for a sign of Francis Hinkel. She saw Teddy doing it too. He went up to Petal and asked boldly, "Where's your fiancé tonight?"

Petal looked down her nose at him as if she didn't understand English. "Who?" she asked haughtily.

Teddy was just as haughty. "Officer Hinkel."

"Oh, him," Petal said, and her cheeks reddened. "On duty, I suppose. Who cares?"

Teddy threw Martha a bewildered look and she shrugged back. Luckily Jemima had been too preoccupied with her hair to remember her bracelet.

Martha was surprised that Mrs. Winterrab was going to join the carolers. She thought for sure she'd be too busy to come, like Mrs. Plum, who had to stay in the kitchen to watch the dinner. She was even more surprised to see her squeeze Teddy's hand before taking charge of the group of guests.

"Now, are we all here? Has everyone got a candle and a songbook?" She looked around with a beaming smile, then frowned. Jemima cringed and checked her hat again. But that wasn't it. "Ah, Mr. Grayly is not down yet," Mrs. Winterrab said, sounding more like her cold, efficient self. "Perhaps someone would be good enough to go up to assist him?"

"No need, here I am," Mr. Grayly said from the stairs. He was wearing a top hat and a black overcoat and looked a bit like Scrooge, except more benevolent.

He apologized for keeping them waiting. "Couldn't be helped, though. Someone was in the bathroom all afternoon."

Jemima quickly grabbed her candle and ran out without getting it lit. The other carolers followed as Jemima led them up the street. The snow that had started that afternoon was still gently falling, in big flakes that made pretty patterns on your clothes or the street before dissolving.

Martha and Teddy waited for Mr. Grayly, who moved slowly and held his candle carefully and refused a carol book because he said he knew all the carols by heart. Teddy made sure the door was locked.

The group stopped at the first house and gave a rousing rendition of "God Rest Ye, Merry Gentlemen." Martha had to admit, Teddy was right. Singing carols put you in a good mood. She forgot she was tired or even cold. And anyway, at each house the people came out and offered them cups of hot apple or cranberry juice sprinkled with cinnamon.

Martha sort of lost track of Teddy and she had to keep reminding herself to find him, because she knew he was watching out for the guests, especially Mr. Grayly, as his mother had told him to do. Poor Teddy. The hotel business didn't let you relax even for a moment.

Some of the narrow streets were dark, and Mrs. Winterrab cautioned everyone to be careful. Suddenly, Teddy was beside Martha.

"Have you noticed anything?" he asked.

Martha was perplexed. "Lots of things. What did you have in mind?"

"I think that kid from town is following us."

Martha peered around but couldn't see much besides the group of carolers and the lighted windows of the houses. "It's a free country," she said. "Maybe he's enjoying the singing . . . or wants to join in."

"No, he doesn't."

"Well, how would you know?"

"Because I know," Teddy said.

Martha was missing out on the singing. They were doing "Silent Night" now, her favorite. "Mrs. Plum would say stuff and nonsense," Martha told him. "You'd better go see if Mr. Grayly's okay. He's fallen way behind."

Even in the dim light Martha could see that Teddy was torn between doing his hotel duty and staying to explain to her further. That was the way Teddy was sometimes. He wanted to tell you the whole story but you had to drag it out of him. For some reason he seemed afraid of the kid from town.

"Go on." She shooed him, and joined the singers only in time for the final verse. The people of the house came out with trays of hot punch and everybody wished each other a Merry Christmas.

"We'll be starting back now," Mrs. Winterrab announced. They had made a wide circle of the streets near the hotel. She directed them down a shortcut, standing guard as they went past, to collect their burned-down candles. She's counting everybody up, like a prison guard, making sure nobody's escaped, Martha thought nastily, coming along at the end and dropping her candle stub into the bag Mrs. Winterrab was holding open.

"Oh . . . Martha, hon?" Mrs. Winterrab said.

Martha was stunned. "Yes?" she managed to croak out.

"Have you seen Teddy? And Mr. Grayly? Where are they?" She peered into the dark and then, frowning and making a *tsk* with her lips, she dug into her shoulder purse and pulled out a pair of glasses. "I hope they aren't lost."

Mrs. Winterrab looked completely different with her glasses on. Glasses could make people look scarier, sort of overly smart and stern. But her glasses made Mrs. Winterrab look all sweet and homey. It was amazing.

"Teddy wouldn't get lost," Martha told her, feeling more eager to be of help. "Maybe he took Mr. Grayly home the other way. I think he was getting tired."

"He's a dear man," Mrs. Winterrab said. "I hope this wasn't too much for him. But Teddy would have told me if they were going back before the rest of us. Oh, my, where is my boy? I depend on him so. I hope nothing's happened."

Martha felt terribly ashamed. Mrs. Winterrab was acting just like a real mother. Just like her own mom and dad would act if Martha suddenly disappeared in the dark, just like that nutty fortune-teller woman had acted about her cats.

"Should I go and look?"

"Oh, goodness, no, not alone. I don't want you getting lost too. But will you walk up the street with me to see if they've stopped to rest?" She called out to the others to go on ahead and said Martha was helping her for a moment. "We don't want to upset anybody," she whispered to Martha, and gave her hand a squeeze just the way she had squeezed Teddy's hand back at the hotel. Martha had certainly been wrong about Mrs. Winterrab.

As it turned out, they found Teddy and Mr. Grayly right away. Mrs. Winterrab was ecstatic and gave both of them a bear hug. She was so happy that nothing had happened that she kept her glasses on all the way back to the hotel and only remembered to snatch them off when she got inside the door.

What she didn't notice was that Teddy was looking very worried. Or maybe she did notice and thought it was because Mr. Grayly had gotten so tired. She bustled everyone to the dining room, where Mrs. Plum had already set out the shrimp cocktails at each place. Teddy sat at Martha's table with her family. Jemima refused to take her hat off and when Teddy started to ask about it, Martha had to give him a warning kick.

In a moment Petal appeared, to serve the roast beef. She scowled as she plunked the plates down, almost tipping the gravy into Dad's lap.

Dad raised his eyebrows. "Something wrong, Petal?"

"Only what can be expected in moogly times, Mr. Lewis," she replied, and marched off to serve more dinners.

Dad looked around the table. "Moogly?"

"Just an old supersition, Mr. Lewis," Teddy said. "You know how the help is these days."

"Well," Dad said, "moogly times or not, this looks delicious."

"Did you give her that message from Officer Hinkel yet?" Martha whispered to Teddy.

"Are you kidding? Why should I deliver messages to that traitor? Besides, I wouldn't go near her when she's in that mood."

Jemima asked to be excused before dessert.

"Don't you dare monopolize that bathroom again," Mom warned.

It wasn't until after dessert that Martha found out what had been bothering Teddy. It was about Mr. Grayly, all right, but not what Martha had thought.

"Remember that weird kid from town? He *was* lurking around—and when he got me alone, he told me one of his thingies."

"Thingies?" Martha asked.

"That's what he calls it. He says, 'I've got a thingie to tell you,' and starts on some crazy story, like his adventures with lions. It's sort of scary, even though I know it's a bunch of lies. Like where would he ever meet up with lions? But tonight . . ." Teddy looked worried. "I don't know . . . I think I might have to believe him."

"What did he tell you?" Martha asked impatiently.

Teddy paused and looked around to be sure no one else would hear.

"He said Mr. Grayly was the one who stole Jemima's bracelet."

Martha scoffed. "How could he even know who Mr. Grayly was?"

"He doesn't. He just said it was the old man in the tall hat."

It was hard to imagine Mr. Grayly as a thief. "Well, you said he's a liar, so why worry about this?"

"That's not the point, Marth!" Teddy cried. "The point is—how did he even know about Jemima's bracelet in the first place?"

"I never thought of that."

"See? So, maybe it's true."

"What do you think we should do? Get Officer Hinkel to arrest him?" Martha asked.

Teddy groaned. "My mother loves Mr. Grayly; he's one of her best guests. He promised to come back and spend the whole summer and bring his sister and cousins too. Think of all the money we'll lose! Oh, boy, my mother is going to blow a fit."

"Calm down," Martha said. "Maybe we can do a little undercover investigating ourselves before we get Officer Hinkel involved."

"Gee, Marth, do you think so?"

"Have we ever failed before?"

"Let's check it out!"

They shook hands on it.

12.

They had a special investigation meeting early the next morning in Martha's room. Right away it was obvious they were split down the middle on their ideas about the case. Teddy was for ghosts and Martha was for facts.

"But it's so creepy," Teddy argued. "That kid just seems to pop up out of nowhere and then disappears. He's never in school."

"Maybe he goes to a private school."

Teddy shook his head. "He's definitely not the type. And anyway, there's only one private school and they wear uniforms. This kid is world-class ratty, even dirty, and . . ."

"And?"

"Well, it's not only the way he dresses. There's something wrong with his face, but I don't know exactly what it is."

"Funny looking? Ugly?" Martha tried to help.

"Not exactly. More like his skin doesn't fit over his bones or something. And he's got this expression, like he knows something I don't."

"Maybe his mother spoils him. Spoiled brats always look smug."

"Well, his mother sure doesn't care how he's dressed. No, I think . . . maybe it's because he's not a real kid."

"You're not going to tell me he's a ghost?"

"No." Teddy hesitated. "But what if somebody changed him, like the cats?"

Martha laughed. "You mean he was a cat that got turned into a boy? Come on, Ted. Those cats were cats and that kid is a kid."

Teddy pouted. "Okay, Martha, your turn."

Martha told him to take notes. "Fact number one: Jemima's bracelet is missing—either misplaced or stolen, we don't know for sure. Fact number two: this kid told you that Mr. Grayly was the thief. That's either true or false, we don't know for sure."

Teddy looked at his pad. "So far, it's a tie between facts and don't-know-for-sures."

"Sooner or later we'll come up with a deciding factor. Let's just keep listing what we know."

"Okay," Teddy said. "Fact number three: I asked the fortune-teller doll to tell me who stole the bracelet. And I did get an answer that night from the kid, which I have already written down as fact number two. I think that adds up to fact number four: The supernatural is at work."

"The supernatural is a don't-know-for-sure, not a fact."

"An investigator should keep an open mind."

"My mind is open! You did ask the fortune-teller and you did get an answer . . . eventually. But that doesn't mean there's a connection."

As soon as Martha said it, she realized she was

76

wrong. There had to be a connection. But she still wasn't willing to believe it was a supernatural one.

"Maybe they're all in it together," she said, thinking aloud.

"Who?"

"The fortune-teller doll, the kid, and Mr. Grayly."

Teddy frowned. "If Mr. Grayly is part of the gang, why would the kid snitch on him?"

"Criminals double-cross each other all the time."

Teddy was unconvinced. "All right, you don't agree with my theory of the supernatural. Then it follows that the doll has no powers but is just a machine. So there definitely is someone else involved. But not Mr. Grayly. We forgot about that funny woman who opened the door. She seems more logical. It's probably her voice that makes the doll talk."

Even though Teddy expounded like a courtroom lawyer, which could get on your nerves, Martha had to agree with him. "Right, that's the way they make money. Remember what Mrs. Plum said, about fools? They get you to put in a penny and then ask for silver. I guess you could get hooked on it and keep coming back for more if you believed you could really see into the future." She looked at Teddy. "You'd probably be one of their best customers."

Ignoring that, Teddy said, "When we snuck in and I asked about the bracelet, they overheard me. So they knew it was a silver bracelet and it was Jemima's."

"But for some reason the doll wasn't working that afternoon. So they had to send the kid to tell you."

They beamed at each other. Then Martha frowned.

77

"No good. They didn't make any money on the deal, so why did they bother?"

"To get us hooked, like you said! To make us believe the doll has powers. Or, maybe, there's a small, puny, little shrimpy possibility of the supernatural being involved after all?"

"There is absolutely nothing supernatural about Jemima's bracelet."

"I still don't think Mr. Grayly really stole it. He looks so innocent and he's far too old to be a thief."

"You can't tell a book by its cover," Martha intoned. "He might have aged from a life of crime. What we need to do is search his room for the evidence."

"That won't be easy. Only Petal is supposed to go into people's rooms to change the linen and clean. If we ask her to look for the bracelet, she'll just blab to Francis."

"You're friends with Mr. Grayly. You keep him busy downstairs and I'll do it."

Ted looked dubious. "If you get caught . . ."

"I'll be extra careful."

"I'm only agreeing because it's a chance to prove that Mr. Grayly is innocent, okay?"

They were too nervous to eat. Mrs. Plum was doing her usual twenty-five things at once, so she didn't notice they only picked at their breakfasts. Tonight was Christmas Eve and the tree-trimming party, and she was busy with the party food.

"Finger sandwiches and little cakes," she said, "so everyone keeps up their appetites for Christmas dinner tomorrow."

Teddy rolled one of his fingers up in a slice of bread and pretended to munch on it. While Mrs. Plum laughed and called him "such a card," Martha managed to sneak their plates over to the sink.

Suddenly, Mrs. Plum's happy expression clouded. "I do hope Petal cheers up in time for the party. She's been walking around with a face like a dead mackerel."

"I noticed she wasn't very festive," Teddy said. "What's the matter with her?"

"Stuff and nonsense about Francis, I expect. Now you two run along, I have work to do."

At first it seemed as if everything was conspiring to keep Martha out of Mr. Grayly's room. Just as she neared the door, Jemima rushed out of the bathroom with a towel on her head and said she thought most of the dye was off but would Martha please check the back?

"Except for some green spots on your neck, it looks fine," Martha assured her. She didn't mention that Jemima's hair now had the texture of a horse's tail.

That done, she again made her way toward Mr. Grayly's door. Just as she was about to turn the knob, Petal popped out of the room.

" 'Morning," she said absently, staring at the fingers of her left hand and wiggling them as she went away.

Phew. A close call. Martha waited a few seconds until Petal went downstairs—but wouldn't you know it, Mom appeared, asking her to please check to see if Jemima had left hair balls in the sink again; people were complaining.

Of course Jemima left hair balls, what else? Martha

cleaned them out and then, finally, she was able to slip into Mr. Grayly's room.

She felt bad about looking through all his stuff. It wasn't a very nice thing to do. She kept telling herself it was for a good cause, but it didn't make her feel better. Mr. Grayly was a very neat man. Everything was tidy. His clothes were hung up, his handkerchiefs squarely folded in the dresser, his slippers lined up under the bed. It was the slippers that got her. Gosh, she'd feel bad if Mr. Grayly really was a thief, she thought as she tipped each slipper over to see if the bracelet was hidden in the toe. She wondered if Officer Hinkel ever felt this way. She decided then and there that she was much too softhearted to ever join the police force.

She looked everywhere she thought a bracelet might be hidden: in drawers, the closet, behind radiators, under chairs and the mattress. Nothing.

She found Mr. Grayly and Teddy in the parlor, playing a game of Scrabble. Teddy looked up with a hopeful, anxious expression.

"You got your wish," she said to him.

Teddy grinned. "Told you so."

"Good morning, Martha," said Mr. Grayly.

"Good morning, Mr. Grayly."

"I'm so glad you've come," he said, shifting a little in his chair. "I was hoping to see you or your sister. I've got something for you."

A Christmas present from Mr. Grayly! She hadn't thought to get him anything, not even a card. It made her feel triple bad about poking through all his private stuff. She hoped she didn't look guilty.

Mr. Grayly reached into the pocket of his slacks. He brought out a silver-and-turquoise bracelet.

He smiled apologetically. "I'm afraid I've forgotten which one of you this belongs to. Do give it to Jemima with my compliments, if it's hers."

Teddy gasped. "Where'd you get that?"

Mr. Grayly looked puzzled. "The trouble is, you see, I really don't know."

13.

Mr. Grayly was upset by his lapse of memory. He said he hoped they wouldn't think him an old coot who couldn't remember his own name, but he had no idea how the bracelet got into his overcoat pocket. One thing he was sure of: It hadn't been there when he was dressing to go caroling the night before.

"Somebody put it there on purpose," Martha said, figuring out what might have happened. That weird kid had been skulking around the carolers. Mr. Grayly had fallen behind. It would only take a moment to drop the bracelet into the pocket and then give Teddy a message. Nothing supernatural about it. The question was how had the kid gotten his hands on the bracelet in the first place?

"Your memory is fine," she told Mr. Grayly. "It was just a very dirty trick."

He continued to look distressed. "Thank you, Martha," he said. "But I'm not so sure my mind is all it could be. In fact, it's my mind that seems to be playing the tricks these days." He hesitated, then lowered his voice. "I've seen some very queer things lately."

Probably Jemima with her red-and-green hair, Martha thought. "What things?"

Mr. Grayly seemed embarrassed. "Do you believe in ghosts?"

"We sure do!" Teddy piped up, ready to tell the whole story of the house they'd unhaunted back in Melody Woods.

"What kind of ghosts?" Martha wanted to know. She remembered Mr. Grayly peering at her through the crack in the door. Had she assumed his innocence a little too soon?

"Just one ghost. I saw it creeping in the upstairs hall. I'm sure it was a ghost because one minute it was there and the next minute it had disappeared into thin air. A smallish ghost," Mr. Grayly said. "Very dark and shabby."

"Funny kind of ghost," Teddy mused. "They're usually invisible or dressed in white sheets."

"This one was dressed in the week's dirty laundry," Mr. Grayly said, and managed a laugh.

"Hey," said Martha. "Would you repeat that, please?"

"Dirty laundry?"

"Ted," Martha said, "describe that weird kid to me."

She listened and heard an exact description of the strange thing she'd seen on the beach the first two mornings she'd been at the hotel. The same thing that had followed them that morning on the boardwalk. Mr. Grayly agreed that Ted's description fit the apparition he had seen himself.

"There's your thief," Martha said to Ted. "The morning Jemima noticed her bracelet was gone was the morning I saw the drape moving in front of the attic stairs. The kid took the bracelet and then slipped behind the drape when he heard me come out of the bathroom."

"You mean he just walked right into the hotel?" Teddy was indignant.

"The door's unlocked during the day. He just sneaked upstairs when he knew everyone was having breakfast. He's as slippery as an eel."

Martha could almost see Teddy's mind racing into a hotel-business mode, figuring out a new security system.

"I may have to speak to my mother about this after all," he said gloomily. "Maybe other guests have had things stolen. We have to do something about that kid."

"You two really don't think I took the bracelet, then?" Mr. Grayly asked. He smiled with relief when they said no.

"I'm so glad. I can't tell you what a help you've been."

"Maybe you could help us," Martha said slowly. "If you're up to it."

Mr. Grayly slapped his knee. "I'm up to anything now that I know I'm not losing my memory!"

"What? What?" Teddy asked.

Thinking fast on her feet, Martha outlined her plan.

14.

It was a race against time, Teddy said. Because if they didn't catch the kid right away, he'd have to tell his mother to lock the door days as well as nights. She'd want to know why and he'd have to explain. That and the possibility of Officer Hinkel showing up.

"We have to do it before the party tonight," he said. "Otherwise, Christmas will be spoiled."

"Your mother's not that bad," Martha said, feeling warmer toward Mrs. Winterrab since she'd put on her glasses the other night. "She wouldn't ruin everyone's Christmas."

"Not everyone's," Teddy lamented. "Just mine. She'll be mad as a hornet that I didn't tell her right away."

"She depends on you, Ted," Martha said kindly. "I'm sure she'll be glad you took over. One less problem for her to solve."

"Maybe."

The plan was to find out what was going on behind the wooden door with the bird knocker. Was the cat woman the kid's mother? Did she know he'd stolen the bracelet? If they realized they had been found out, they might be scared off. Hadn't Officer Hinkel said the boardwalk was full of fly-by-nights? Martha hoped that's what the kid and his mother would do. Then Ted could tell Officer Hinkel it had all been a mistake. Jemima had her bracelet back and nothing else had been stolen. Teddy had found that out by cleverly asking his mother in a roundabout way. "I'm proud of our spotless reputation," she had said, which, of course, made Teddy feel awful.

They had to persuade Jemima to help too. Martha was worried about sending Mr. Grayly alone, and she couldn't accompany him because the cat woman would recognize her.

Luckily, Jemima was in an ecstatic mood because not only had the dye come out of her hair but Mellow had sent her a last-minute Christmas card. It was a mushy one, too, Martha knew, because Jemima blushed and hid it right away. Getting her bracelet back was nothing compared to getting a card from Mellow. Her brain was so addled because of some soppy card, she would have done anything.

The plan was this: Teddy would set himself up as a decoy, to attract the kid's attention. The kid was sure to grab the opportunity to talk to Teddy and, this time, Teddy wouldn't run away.

While Ted and the kid discussed "thingies" and lion's teeth, Mr. Grayly and Jemima would go to the fortune-teller's door and ask to have their fortunes told by the mechanical doll. That way, they could find out quickly if the woman and the kid were running a fortune-telling scam. If not, they would still find an excuse to talk to her. In any case, they would get the conversation around to her son and let her know that it was only a matter of time before the police were on to him about the stolen bracelet. But, if she and her son would agree to pack up and leave town, nothing more would be said.

Martha, Teddy, Jemima, and Mr. Grayly met in the empty dining room after lunch. The other guests had either gone for walks or up to their rooms for naps. Mrs. Winterrab was in her office, and Mrs. Plum and Petal were busy in the kitchen, preparing for the party. Through the closed door could be heard the barking of Mrs. Plum's orders and Petal's sulky replies. Petal was still in a very bad mood.

They went over every step of the plan, backward and forward.

"Don't forget not to wear the bracelet," Teddy reminded Jemima. "We want to set a trap and make sure it works."

Jemima stuck out her bare wrists. "Don't you and Martha forget to come and rescue Mr. Grayly and me if we get stuck in there too long."

"I've got a weapon, just in case," Mr. Grayly said, and produced his big black furled umbrella with the heavy wood handle. He gave it a menacing shake. "Hasn't let me down yet."

"I guess that's it. We're ready," Martha said. Her job was to be commander of the entire operation. She had to be everywhere at once.

15.

At first everything went according to plan. Martha watched from behind a dune as Teddy dawdled in front of some closed shops and Mr. Grayly and Jemima pretended to be taking the air on the boardwalk.

Out of nowhere, just like a ghost, came the raggedy specimen they had hoped for. He scuttled up to Teddy and as soon as Martha saw they were engaged in serious conversation, she gave the signal.

Jemima and Mr. Grayly immediately proceeded down the boardwalk to the fortune-teller's door, Mr. Grayly walking in his usual careful way and Jemima gently trying to hurry him along. But they got there in good time, Martha was relieved to see. The kid was still chewing Teddy's ear off.

She saw Jemima lift the bird-shaped knocker. There was a long pause and Martha's heart sank. But then the door opened and the square woman stood glaring at them. Martha could almost read her lips asking, "Whatta you want?"

Teddy and the kid were still talking, but Martha noticed that Teddy was moving subtly backward, one step at a time. The kid, deep in conversation, didn't seem to notice that they were moving toward the boardwalk.

Timing was crucial. Ted had to delay long enough for Jemima and Mr. Grayly to get to the important moment. This was when Jemima would accuse the cat woman's son of stealing her silver bracelet. The kid would burst in, see Mr. Grayly, and accuse him of the theft. Mr. Grayly, putting on an act like he was absent-minded, would deny it. Unable to resist, the kid would tell them to look in the old man's overcoat pocket.

"Aha!" Martha would say, coming in. "How did you know it was in his pocket?"

All would be lost for the thieving pair and they'd pack up and leave.

At least that's the way she imagined it happening, like a movie taking place in her mind.

But in the real-life version a few things changed.

Teddy and the kid, still talking, began walking down the boardwalk to the door. Martha moved along underneath, keeping pace with the sound of their footsteps overhead. It was cold and damp under the boardwalk, and it smelled of dead fish. But she pushed on as a commander should.

When she figured they were just about even with the wooden door, she popped her head up. Ted and the kid were nowhere to be seen. But there, in front of her, stood Officer Hinkel.

"Oh . . . hi," Martha said. "I was just . . . exploring. . . ." She gave him a winning smile.

Officer Hinkel's very blue eyes looked out to sea. "I've heard rumors about some kind of undercover operation going on," he said casually, as if he weren't really talking to her at all.

"Really?" Martha said, trying to keep her own eyes on Officer Hinkel and not on the wooden door.

"Could be dangerous."

"Everything's under control," Martha said.

"We don't know that."

"We don't?" Martha thought about it. They'd been in there a long time. Was Mr. Grayly beating them over the head with his umbrella yet? "No, I guess we don't."

"Why don't we check it out?" Officer Hinkel suggested.

For an awful moment she was afraid he was going to take her hand and lead her off to the police station. But he walked over to the wooden door and gave two hard raps on the knocker. "Open up—police!"

It was the raggedy kid who opened the door. He and Martha stared at each other, eye to eye, and then he craned his neck to look up at Officer Hinkel. "Come on in and join the party," he said.

Martha saw right away what Teddy had meant about something being weird. The kid just didn't seem like a kid, not in the way he spoke to Officer Hinkel or in the way he stood back to let them in. But he was kid-sized and skinny. Martha got up her courage and peered at him closely as she walked past. He had wrinkles!

They went down the hall to the room where Teddy, Jemima, Mr. Grayly, and the cat woman were standing in front of the case that held the fortune-telling doll. Officer Hinkel sneezed.

"I guess you know most of these folks," the kid said. "But let me introduce myself: I'm Leo the Lion Tamer, and this is my wife, Flo."

Martha gasped.

"Yeah, he's not a kid after all," Teddy said. He scowled at Officer Hinkel. "What's he doing here?"

"He was just . . . here," Martha said.

"Good thing too," said Mr. Grayly. "This is far too confusing. We need someone official to get at the truth."

Everybody started talking at once. The fortune-teller doll just stood in her case, with her head cocked, giving them a glittery black-eyed stare. Finally Officer Hinkel called for quiet. Everybody shut up.

Slowly, in an orderly fashion, the story came out.

Leo began. "As I was saying before, I found the bracelet after I saw her—Jemima she says her name is —jogging on the beach. I only wanted to return it. The door was open, so I went in. Everyone is busy eating breakfast. Nobody at the desk. What's the harm in having a look around? What a fancy place! I go upstairs, in all innocence, believe me, and I run into trouble." He pointed to Martha and then to Mr. Grayly. "This one in the bathroom and that one coming out his door. I acted on pure instinct. Hid behind the drapes."

Officer Hinkel looked skeptical. "Why hide if you were innocent?" he asked, and sneezed.

"Because I knew they'd get me wrong!" Leo cried. "People always get me wrong. Take this boy—Ted he says his name is. He looked an interesting sort of person, for a kid. Flo says we should lay low so people won't ask questions. That's hard for a friendly type like me. So I figure, what's the harm in talking to a kid? All I wanted was a little chat. But every time he sees me, he runs the other way. Except for today. I should have smelled a rat."

"We didn't do anything wrong," Flo wailed, unable to keep quiet any longer. "All we wanted was a nice place to stay the winter." She glared at her husband. "It was his stupid idea to fool around with that contraption." She gave the glass case a kick and the fortune-teller doll rocked a little.

"My idea!" Leo shouted. "It was your scheme from the start. Make a little extra money. Look where it got us."

"You should talk," Flo yelled back. "Why'd you stick your nose where it didn't belong, Mr. Big Talker?"

When they realized the rest were staring at them, they stopped arguing. Leo's mouth drooped.

"We've fallen on hard times," he said plaintively. "Used to be with the International Circus. Flo was the queen of the trapeze. I was the world's smallest lion tamer. The lions got old and lost their teeth. Animal-rights people took offense." He singled Martha out to plead his case. "I never really whipped them. It was all for show. Bunch of big babies they were." He looked around. "Now all I have are these mangy cats. Nastier than any lions." As if to prove him right, one of the cats spat and lashed out with a claw.

Officer Hinkel put an efficient stop to the palaver. "I think you'd better come down to the station," he said to Flo and Leo.

Leo bristled. "What's the charge?"

Officer Hinkel smiled. "Take your choice: trespassing, squatting, fortune-telling without a license . . ."

"Not stealing, though. I never stole the bracelet."

"Then why didn't you return it the day you came to the hotel?" Martha asked.

"I got scared and it went clear out of my head. I did go back, but everybody was coming out carrying a candle. I saw an opportunity and slipped it in that old duffer's pocket."

Mr. Grayly frowned.

"Figured he might not know what to do with it, so I gave Ted here a tip."

Teddy looked at Leo with disapproval. "You told me Mr. Grayly had stolen the bracelet. That wasn't fair."

Leo looked remorseful. "No, I guess that wasn't."

"I'll get my coat," Flo said. "Come on, Leo, we'd better cooperate."

"Good idea," said Officer Hinkel.

"Umm . . ." Jemima said as they started out the door. "Ummmm . . ."

Martha gave her a poke.

"Ummm, I think I should say something."

Everybody stopped.

"I think I should say that Mr. Leo could be right. I might have lost my bracelet on the beach."

"But Jemima, you said . . ." Martha began.

"Now's a fine time to tell us," Teddy joined in.

"I really don't remember if I was wearing it that morning or not," Jemima explained. "I mean, it could've been stolen, I just don't know for sure. But I wouldn't want someone getting into trouble because of that."

Martha groaned.

Officer Hinkel said he would take it into consideration but that didn't eliminate all the charges. He escorted Leo and Flo to the door.

"What about these cats?" Martha called.

"Call the shelter to come and give them a merry Christmas," Francis Hinkel said, and sneezed again.

Martha was the last one out of the room. She looked back at the fortune-telling doll. It stood there, motionless, black eyes full of secrets it would never tell. Martha wondered if it was her imagination, or had the doll cocked its head to the *other* side? She turned around and ran out, telling herself it was really silly to have thought she'd heard the beginnings of a whir.

16.

The tree-trimming party was a big success. Mrs. Winterrab surprised them by bringing out two big boxes of very old decorations.

"I've been hiding these in the attic," she said.

Everybody helped put the ornaments on the tree, then threw tinsel all over it and each other. Everyone was in the best of moods, embracing and kissing and wishing each other a very Merry Christmas. Martha felt really happy when she saw Mrs. Winterrab give Teddy a big hug.

Even Petal looked in a better mood with tinsel all over her head. But Martha noticed her eyes were red.

Teddy noticed too. "Maybe she's sorry she blabbed to Francis about us," he said to Martha. "I guess I should tell her it's all right, seeing it's Christmas Eve and all."

"That would be nice, Ted."

They went over and Teddy told Petal she had done the right thing by not asking Francis to go under cover.

Petal was astonished. "But I did tell him to do exactly that." Her eyes narrowed. "Why, what did he do?"

"Don't be mad at him," Ted said hastily. "He actually came to the rescue in the nick of time."

"A true policeman." Petal sighed and looked ready to cry.

"Well . . ." Ted fumbled. "What's wrong, then?"

Petal drew herself up and wiped her eyes. "I suppose it doesn't matter if you know. I should have known myself, seeing as how it's moogly times. But here it is. I told Francis I wouldn't walk out with him another time until he produced a ring." She fluttered her ringless left hand. "How can you feel you're engaged if you don't have a ring?"

"Maybe it costs too much money for a policeman," Martha offered.

"I don't care what kind of ring it is," Petal said. "It's the principle of the thing. I told him that, the same day I told him about going under cover for you." Petal's eyes spilled over again. "I wouldn't care if it was a bubble-gum-machine ring!"

Martha looked at Teddy with sudden realization. Teddy went pale. "Er, Petal—I think we forgot to give you an important message from Francis. You see, we were—"

At that moment there was a sudden flurry as the front door opened, setting the Christmas ornaments tinkling and fluttering the tinsel so it looked like magical snow.

"Look, everyone, it's Santa," Mrs. Winterrab cried.

Santa was very tall and he had the bluest eyes Martha had ever seen. He smiled a very bright smile through his cotton beard as he began to pass out the gifts from his big red sack. When he got to Petal he gave her a very small box.

Martha knew what was in it, even before she saw the diamond wink in the light of the Christmas candles.

Moogly times were neither good nor bad, she thought. Things happened because of people, not frozen waves. People got things wrong a lot, of course. But in their hearts they really wanted everything to be right.

And right now people were making it the best, most wonderful moogly Christmas of all.

Masterful mysteries by

PHYLLIS REYNOLDS NAYLOR

Winner of the Edgar Allan Poe Award

☐ **NIGHT CRY**   40017-1 $3.25
Scaredy-cat Ellen Stump really has something
to worry about when a suspicious stranger
starts hanging around her house just after a
local boy is kidnapped

☐ **THE WITCH HERSELF**   40044-9 $2.95
Lynn and her best friend Mouse are terrified
when Lynn's mother sets up an office in the
home of a dangerous witch!

☐ **THE WITCH'S SISTER**   40028-7 $2.95
Lynn is convinced her sister, Judith, is a witch—
especially after she sees her conjure up a real
live boy from the middle of a lake!

☐ **WITCH WATER**   40038-4 $2.95
Lynn and Mouse are off on another
witch hunt—only this time it's a spooky
old neighbor that they're after...